NOBODY'S CAT

NOBODY'S CAT

by Miska Miles

Illustrated by John Schoenherr

An Atlantic Monthly Press Book

TORONTO   Little, Brown and Company   BOSTON

Other Books by Miska Miles

KICKAPOO	FOX AND THE FIRE
DUSTY AND THE FIDDLERS	TEACHER'S PET
SEE A WHITE HORSE	RABBIT GARDEN
PONY IN THE SCHOOLHOUSE	THE PIECES OF HOME
MISSISSIPPI POSSUM	UNCLE FONZO'S FORD

ATLANTIC-LITTLE, BROWN BOOKS
ARE PUBLISHED BY
LITTLE, BROWN AND COMPANY
IN ASSOCIATION WITH
THE ATLANTIC MONTHLY PRESS

Published simultaneously in Canada
by Little, Brown & Company (Canada) Limited

PRINTED IN THE UNITED STATES OF AMERICA

For Fern Harvey

Born in an old box in a narrow alley, the cat knew many things about the city. He knew about trucks and dogs. And he knew about people. He knew when to run. And he knew when to walk without fear.

In the nights, he heard the thud of heavy feet hurrying along the sidewalk, the whine of tires in the street, doors slamming in the alley.

Often in the days, he stalked the length of his alley to a loading platform, for on this platform, behind a pile of old barrels, was a box half full of papers, where he slept.

This late afternoon, he jumped from his box and stretched until he felt long and comfortable. Then he started out to hunt for his food.

On a fire escape, a girl sat with her hands locked together around her knees.

Music rocked from a high window. The cat stopped under the fire escape and called softly, but the girl did not hear him.

He went on, along his alley.

5

He saw an open window close to the ground.

He jumped to the sill and sat there.

Inside, there was no sound.

On silent paws, he let himself down to the floor and sniffed the linoleum. When he found nothing to eat, he leaped to the sill again, and dropped to the alley.

Beside a door, a fat gray cat with white feet sat drinking from a saucer.

The scraggly cat smelled milk. He stalked toward the good smell. The gray cat arched his back and hissed threateningly.

They sprang together and they rolled, screaming and biting, thumping and tumbling.

The door clicked open.

"Get out of here," a man shouted.

The fat gray cat released his hold and scuttled through the doorway into the house. The cat ran down the alley and stopped beside a garbage pail.

When the alley was quiet, he licked his leg where it was matted with blood. He flicked his left ear. He flicked it again, and held his head a little to the side.

9

He crept back to the doorway. The saucer, half filled with milk, was still there. And he lapped the good, sweet milk.

With his tail straight and high, he went limping down the alley to the street. He walked in the shadow of the buildings, away from the street lights.

He stopped beside a parked truck and washed his face and his ears. He was careful as he washed his left ear.

When morning came he was still hungry, so he trotted on down the street until he came to a familiar doorway where he smelled meat. He sat there until the door opened and he arched his back and rubbed against a man's leg.

He followed the man inside the shop and waited until the man set a handful of meat scraps on the floor.

After he had eaten, he allowed the man to scratch him on the neck, and then he walked outside and sat down beside the door.

Along the street, shop doors were being opened, voices called—happy voices, impatient voices. Trucks rolled by and buses honked.

13

A huge dog came down the street. The cat sprang up and ran and the dog galloped close behind him.

They raced into an alley and the cat found himself in a corner made by two walls and there was no place to go. He turned to face the dog. The cat hissed. The dog growled and came close—he retreated a step and then lunged forward.

The cat lifted a paw and struck, and the dog reached for the cat, snapping his jaws together.

With a great leap, the cat jumped to the dog's back and clung there.

Yelping, the dog ran down the alley, along a street, across an intersection and the cat loosened his hold and jumped lightly to the sidewalk.

He crouched where he landed beside a fire hydrant. The dog kept running. When he was out of sight, the cat sat bracing his back against the hydrant, and washed his feet.

He walked on, past a laundry, past a grocer's store, on to another safe alley.

When night came again, it grew cold, and in the narrow, dark slit of sky between the tall old brick buildings, lightning flashed. And after a while, thunder rolled and rumbled and the cat felt excited and ran stiff-legged down the alley.

He came to a narrow old house with a rickety back porch. He ran up the steps. Above his head hung a string. It moved slightly in the wind and the cat leaped high into the air. He caught the string and a light flashed on.

Like a wild thing, he slithered off the porch and ran under an old car parked in the narrow driveway. Rain came.

Lightning and thunder flared and rocked again, and the alley ran with water.

The cat crawled out and he jumped through a window of the car into the back seat, and shook the water from his feet. He found a soft, worn place on the cushion where he slept.

In the morning, the storm was over.

21

Someone opened the car door and a man's voice said, "Hurry, Annabelle. You'll be late for school. Wait. Turn that light off when you come. Did you leave it on last night?"

"No, Papa," a girl's voice answered. "I didn't leave it on. I turned it off. Honest."

The cat lay in the back seat without moving, and the car rolled along its way. After a time it stopped.

Quick as a lightning flash, the cat was out of the car.

"A cat was in the car," Annabelle said. "And it's limping."

"It's not limping very much," her father said. "It'll be all right. That cat can take care of itself."

The cat ran through a wide gate and stopped inside a high wire fence.

Boys and girls came through the gate. Some had lunch boxes.

The cat arched his back against the fence and watched them go by.

He watched through the morning and then it was noon. The smell of food came through an open door.

He crossed the pavement to the lunchroom door and stalked inside.

He jumped up on a counter beside a platter of meat. "GET OUT! GET HIM OFF—"

The cat ran around the room and the boys and girls laughed and ran after him.

Outside, the custodian sat on a bench near the school-house, and opened his own lunch box.

A teacher called from the door of the lunchroom, "Mr. Andrews. Please come. There's a wild cat in here."

Mr. Andrews rose slowly. "I'll be right there," he said.

When Mr. Andrews came into the room, the boys and girls were in a half-circle around the cat, and he huddled in a corner, his fur stiff, his ears back, his tail close against his body.

"He's not wild," Mr. Andrews said.

As he reached down, the cat darted between the man's boots. He ran straight through the doorway— on past the bench. But he smelled something good and, cautiously, he returned to the bench.

He reached into the open lunch box and clawed at a chicken leg. He seized it in his sharp teeth and carried it to the gate.

When Mr. Andrews came back, he looked in his lunch box. "Well, Cat," he said. "Maybe you're hungrier than I am."

When the cat finished eating, a boy and a girl crossed over to him.

The boy reached out and touched the cat's ribs with his forefinger, and the cat seized his hand with teeth and claws. The boy didn't move and the cat didn't bite.

When the school yard was empty, the cat went out through the wide gate and stopped at the curb.

Cars rumbled and clattered along beside him, and he waited, waving his tail.

When a space cleared, he stepped into the street. A car came speeding toward him.

For a moment he crouched there, afraid to move. He heard the scream of swerving tires and felt the push of air. As the car hurtled past, he flattened himself against the street. Then he ran, low and fast, to the sidewalk, back through the gate and to the safety of the school yard.

33

That night, the cat prowled around the school yard.

A small brown dog came, and the cat stood waiting.

The dog came close and blew on the cat's head and parted his fur, and the cat was not afraid.

Next morning, the sun came up in a sky of pink and gold. And when the boys and girls came to school, they brought food for the cat.

"I've got fish for him," Annabelle said.

The cat ate until his stomach was round and tight.

Annabelle rubbed his jaw with a gentle finger, and the cat stretched his neck and permitted this.

A bell rang and the cat followed the boys and girls into the school.

Annabelle turned into Room Three and found her own desk and sat down.

The cat jumped up on a long, high desk at the side of the room. He lay on a stack of papers and ruffled the papers with his paw.

"I see we have a cat," the teacher said.

"He's a paperweight cat," Annabelle said.

He stayed in Room Three until school was over that day, and then he went outside and crossed the school yard, slinking like a tiger.

When the moon rose, he saw his own shadow and he jumped sideways, his back arched, his legs straight.

Then he saw a small movement in the weeds outside the fence. Slowly, slowly, he crawled along close to the concrete.

A mouse twitched his whiskers inquiringly.

The cat crouched.

Like a tiger he sprang, and the mouse was his.

When it was limp, he picked it up daintily and carried it to the school, and left it on the top step against the door.

He stalked out through the gate and along the sidewalk, close to the fence.

Feet clicked and hurried along the walk. A small dog saw the cat. Yelping, he leaned hard against his leash, his front feet pawing the air.

Just beyond reach of the dog, the cat watched, the end of his tail twitching only slightly.

When the feet and the dog were gone, the cat padded on his way. On and on he went. Unerringly, he found familiar places, until finally he turned into the dark jungle of his own alley.

He trotted straight to the loading platform and jumped up.

Inside his box, he turned around to make his bed. His claws were out, just enough to scratch the paper. And almost without sound, he purred until he went to sleep.